100 Easy Ways to Teach Your Child to Love God's World

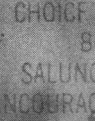

BAKER
A DIVISION OF
Baker Book House Co

FINGERTIP BOOKS

Copyright 1994 by Margaret Houk

Published by Baker Books,
a division of Baker Book House Company
P.O. Box 6287, Grand Rapids, MI 49516-6287

Printed in the United States of America

ISBN: 0-8010-4403-0

All rights reserved. No part of this publication may be reproduced, stored in a retrieval system, or transmitted in any form or by any means—electronic, mechanical, photocopy, recording, or any other—without the prior written permission of the publisher. The only exception is brief quotations in printed reviews.

To have faith is to live with the Lord every moment. God is with us all of the time, in every place. To love him is to see him everywhere, in the everyday things and in the spectacular.

God is to be found in the soft shade of cloudy days as well as in the sunshine that brightens our streets and yards. He is in the serene smile of an elderly woman whose body is frail and mind is fogged as well as in the ecstasy that floods us as we waltz to Mozart or marvel over a Van Gogh.

How do we teach our children to love God's world? We begin by showing them the magnificent world he created, the preciousness of all of its creatures, and the gifts he gives them. To drink in all of these things is to be nourished by the wonder of their maker.

Then, along with our children we grow in our love of the giver of these marvelous gifts. For love is built on appreciation, magnified thousands of times and ways.

Lie on your back in the grass and make up stories about the clouds.

*Hunt for pollywogs
in a creek.*

Go berry picking.

*Travel secondary roads
and stop to look at
the roadside wildflowers.*

*Play with sand.
Shove it around,
sift it,
make soft circles in it
with a finger,
and lie in it.*

Build a walled city with wet sand.

Look for wild roses in June.

Wade in a lake or the ocean.

Look for a school of fish in a lake.

Sit at a seashore and watch the waves roll in.

* * *

Watch an ocean tide come in and go out.

Feed the seagulls at a beach.

Watch undulating meadow grasses wave to and fro.

Note the different colors of the wet pebbles in a creek.

Study a tree: its leaves, trunk, branches, bark, seeds, or nuts or fruit.

Make a weed bouquet.

Study rocks. Note their different colors, patterns, and densities. Then group them by similarities.

Pull apart and study a milkweed pod.

Take a fall color tour.

❋ ❋ ❋

Climb a mountain.

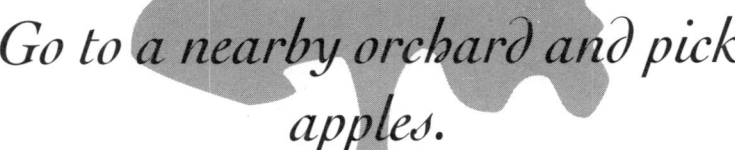

Go to a nearby orchard and pick apples.

Find the continental divide on a map and explain it to your child. If you live near it, find a place where it is marked by signs.

Try to find the source of a river near your home or in your state.

Take a bouquet of flowers from your yard or vegetables from your garden to a lonely, sick, or hurting neighbor.

Turn some rocks over and see what is underneath.

*Watch an airplane take off.
Better yet, go up in an airplane
and look down at the earth.*

Draw with chalk on a sidewalk (where permissible).

Study a snowflake under a magnifying glass.

*Make a homemade sundial.
Place it outdoors and watch
it for a week.*

Take a winter hike in a snowy field and look for weed colors.

Bring a pinecone indoors and watch it open.

*Look for animal tracks
in the snow.*

* * *

Talk about the joy of all seasons.

*Make an angel
in the snow.*

Watch the stars move in the sky. Or take in a planetarium program.

*Look for a chickadee
in a pine tree.*

Visit an art gallery. Look for the distinctive styles of each artist.

Study the blossoms on a fruit tree as it begins to set fruit.

Walk the woods in early spring and look for wildflowers. Bring a book along to identify them.

Take a walk in an orchard and enjoy the fragrant blossoms. Listen for the bees humming among the flowers.

Plant a vegetable garden and watch it grow.

* * *

Chain a dandelion necklace.

*Look for migrating geese.
Note their V-shaped formation.*

Watch a mother bird feed her babies. Use binoculars; getting close will scare them.

Hang some clothes outdoors on a line. When they are dry, smell their freshness.

*Listen to a cardinal's songs.
Cardinals have many majestic
and lyrical melodies and calls.
Can you hear them all.*

Follow the life cycle of a deciduous tree for a year.

Raise animals and watch them mate and give birth. Rabbits are good. They are soft and cuddly to hold, cohabit readily, and can be kept in hutches in the garage. (Don't let the neighbor's cat in!)

Let a child help you cook spaghetti by measuring out the water and spaghetti. Smell the aroma and watch the water boil. Talk about how God provides different kinds of foods all over the world.

Buy an ant farm and study the ant community's activities.

Build a homemade radio.

Talk to a flowering plant for a week and look for a response.

Plant a seed and watch it grow. Or place a sweet potato half or a pineapple top in shallow water in a dish.

Listen to a heartbeat — yours or someone else's.

Buy a magnet and find every-thing in your house that it will attract.

Make bread or other yeast dough and watch it rise.

✻ ✻ ✻

Buy some whipping cream and make butter.

Play with gravity. Gather a collection of items (feather, balloon, piece of leather, spoon). Drop them from waist-high level and count time until they reach the floor.

*Plan a special
"Day with Grandpa."*

*Make up a design
and paint a
T-shirt together.*

Read poems to each other.

✻ ✻ ✻

Sing a song together. Tape it, and listen to the tape.

Go to a mall and watch the people. Study their faces or their different walks.

Visit a dairy farm or an egg farm.

Visit a hospital nursery and look at the newborns. Or, if appropriate, include your child in your family's pregnancy and birth experiences.

Talk to an animal and watch its response.

Help an elderly or disabled person by carrying his or her packages.

Offer your seat on the bus to an elderly, frail, or disabled persons.

Visit a natural history museum.

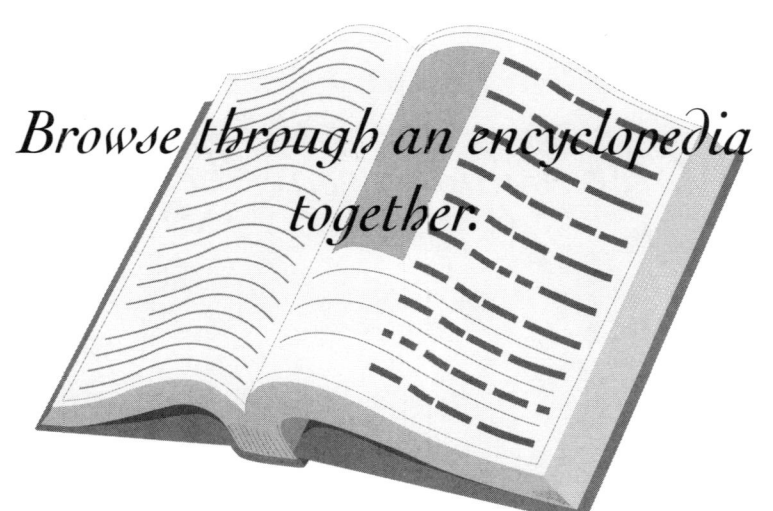

Browse through an encyclopedia together.

Watch a spider weave her web.

When it's raining and the sun comes out, look for the rainbow.

Find plants that are growing between cracks of a rock or pavement.

When you visit Grandma, listen for her "grandma voice."

Put a conch shell to your ear and listen.

Take a walk along a beach and find shells or stones of different colors.

Listen for night sounds anytime, anywhere. The night has a music all its own.

Watch a storm come in.

❋ ❋ ❋

*Take a walk after a storm
and look for earthworms.*

Smile at every person you see within an hour and note the responses.

Listen to the laughter of other children at play.

Watch a sunset. Talk about the visual differences between a sunrise and a sunset.

Make up a story. Take turns filling in the details. Talk about how God inspires our imaginings.

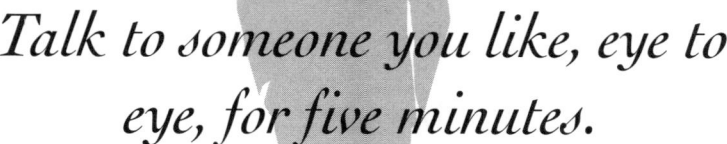

Talk to someone you like, eye to eye, for five minutes.

Say "Good Morning" to God every morning.

Say "Good Night" to God at bedtime.

Tell your child Bible stories in language of today as though they are happening today. (Use pennies instead of farthings, houses instead of tents, etc.) Watch the stories come alive.

Teach your child how to tithe with his or her allowance. Let the child decide where the tithe will go. Visit the site of the tithe gift's destination.

Share one of your "quiet times," use your "sacred space," and meditate together.

Tell your child every day that you love him or her.

Tell your child you love him or her every time that child disobeys.

Love your child by giving him or her your time, attention, and respect. Nothing says "love" better than the doing. Nothing prompts love better than knowing your are loved.

Give your child a pet to love.

❊ ❊ ❊

Give your child a plant to care for.

Take a walk together in the moonlight.

*Hug and kiss your child
at bedtime.
As you leave the room
and turn off the light, say,
"God and I love you!"*